C.

Captains Courageous

by Rudyard Kipling

retold by Alan Venable and Jerry Stemach

Don Johnston Incorporated
Volo, Illinois

Edited by:

Jerry Stemach, MS, CCC-SLP

Gail Portnuff Venable, MS, CCC-SLP

Dorothy Tyack, MA

Consultant:

Ted S. Hasselbring, PhD

Graphics and Illustrations:

Photographs and illustrations are all created professionally
and modified to provide the best possible support for the
intended reader.

Narration:

Professional actors and actresses read the text to build
excitement and to model research-based elements of fluency:
intonation, stress, prosody, phrase groupings and rate.
The rate has been set to maximize comprehension for the reader.

Published by:

Don Johnston Incorporated
26799 West Commerce Drive
Volo, IL 60073

800.999.4660 USA Canada
800.889.5242 Technical Support
www.donjohnston.com

DON JOHNSTON

International Standard Book Number
ISBN 1-4105-0259-7

To courageous captains of land, sea, and air,
and to their courageous crews

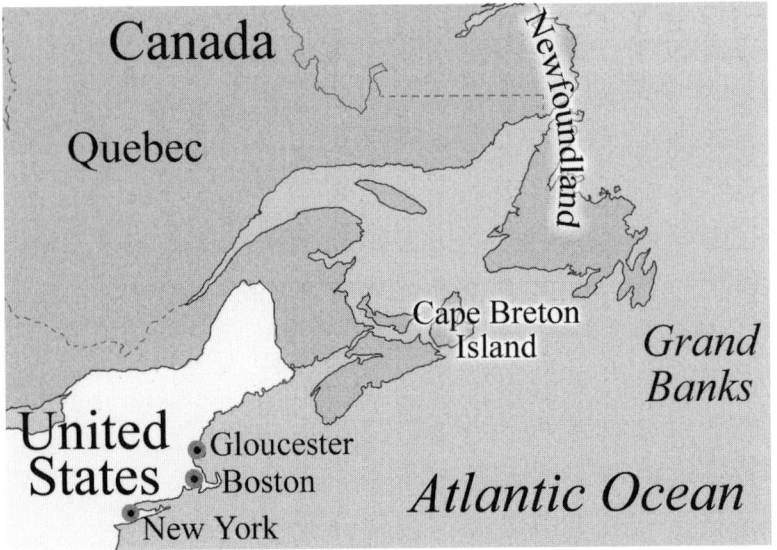

Chapter One

The Rich Boy Drowns

Fog covered the North Atlantic sea. In the rooms of the enormous steamship, the passengers could hear the ship's whistle as it warned smaller boats to get out of its path. The steamship was crossing the Grand Banks, where dozens of boats would be out fishing.

"If you ask me, that millionaire kid is a spoiled brat!" said one of the men aboard the steamship. "He isn't wanted here, that's for certain." *Here* was the "smoking room" where several men had gathered to pass the time.

"I know this kind of boy," said a white-haired German who spoke between bites of a sandwich. "America is full of them. What that boy needs is a few good whippings with a rope!"

"Well, I pity the boy myself," said a man from New York. "What can you expect? His father owns all those millions out West, and his wife can't stand living out there so she drags the boy all over the country, from one rich hotel to another. Now she thinks that she can turn him into a gentleman by taking him to a school in Europe!"

"The boy told me he gets $200 a month to spend any way he pleases," said another man from Philadelphia.

"I heard the old man owns railroads," said the German.

"Yep," the Philadelphia man replied. "And lumber mills and mines and a fleet of ships out in California. He's what you might call a big-time captain of industry. It's a pity he has no time for his son. There's still some good in the boy if you could get at it."

"I'll tell you how to get at it," said the German. "With the end of a rope!"

Just then, the door opened and 15-year-old Harvey Cheyne Junior stepped inside. He was all dressed up in a red jacket and cap, and a half-smoked cigarette hung from his mouth. He looked a little seasick from the rolling of the ship. The door banged open behind him.

"Say, you can hear the fishing boats squawking all around us!" Harvey said in a loud, high voice. "Wouldn't it be great if we ran over one in this fog!"

"Shut the door, Harvey, and stay outside. You're not wanted in here," said the New Yorker.

"Who's gonna stop me? Did any of you pay for my ticket?" Harvey asked, pulling on his cigarette. Seeing that it had gone out, he threw it to the floor. Next, he took out a roll of cash. "Say, gentlemen, how about a game of poker?"

The German grinned wickedly. He opened his cigar-case, handed the boy a long black cigar, and said, "This is the proper thing to smoke, my young friend."

Harvey lit the cigar and said, "It will take more than this to keel me over!" But as he began to puff, his eyes began to water and his face grew pale.

"You like my cigar, eh?" asked the German. All the men laughed.

Harvey mumbled something about "fine flavor." Then he opened the door and staggered out into the fog.

The wet deck was rolling, his head was spinning, and he was fainting from seasickness. At a railing at the end of the deck, his body doubled up with pain. Suddenly he rolled over the railing. He felt his feet floating in the breeze. Then a low, gray wave rose out of the sea, grabbed him and tucked him under its arm.

* * *

Harvey was sure that he had drowned, and yet somehow he could smell salt water, fried fish, burnt grease, paint, and stale tobacco.

When he opened his eyes, he found himself on a hard, narrow bunk with a lamp swinging back and forth overhead.

"Feelin' better?" said a voice.

"Where am I? What happened?"

"Oh, Manuel was out in one of the dories yesterday, and you were the biggest fish he caught! But don't worry. Now you're snug in the bow of a fishing boat called the *We're Here*. She's a first class schooner."

A boy got up from beside a stove at the other end of the narrow room. He was about the same age as Harvey, with a flat red face and twinkling gray eyes. He wore high rubber boots. He held out a tin cup.

"Have some coffee?" said the boy.

"Isn't there milk?" asked Harvey.

"Well, no," said the boy. "Ain't likely to get milk till the middle of September. It ain't bad coffee. I made it myself."

Harvey drank in silence.

"Eat this, then get up on deck," said the boy, handing Harvey a plate of fried pork. "Dad wants to see you. I'm his son, Dan, and I help the cook and do the dirty stuff that the men won't do. I'm glad *you're* here! I haven't had anyone else to help me since Otto fell overboard and drowned."

"What are you talking about?" said Harvey. "I'm not here to help anyone!"

"Maybe not," said Dan. "But right now you better go up on deck, because Dad wants to see you, and he's the captain."

"Listen," said Harvey. "I don't *take* orders. I *give* them. If your dad wants to talk to me, send him down here. And tell him to head this boat back to New York right away. I'll pay him."

Dan's jaw dropped and his eyes lit up. "That's a good one!" he laughed. "Say, Dad!" he called up the open hatch. "The boy says you can come down here if you want to talk to him so bad!"

The answer came back in the deepest voice that Harvey had ever heard. "Quit foolin', Dan, and send him to me."

There was something about the tone of voice that sent Harvey up the ladder.

On deck he saw that the ship was anchored. Off in the distance all around, five or six dories were bobbing around on the waves.

"Good afternoon, young feller," said a short, stocky man with thick, gray eyebrows.

Harvey did not like being called *young feller*. He said, "I demand that you take me back to New York immediately."

The man looked amazed.

"Look, here, my father will pay you as much as you want," said Harvey. "You've probably heard of my father, the millionaire, Mr. Harvey Cheyne. He could buy a thousand dirty boats like yours!"

"Is that so?" said the man.

"Look, I'll pay you myself! I get $200 every month to spend as I please!" Harvey reached in his pocket.

The pocket was empty except for a soggy pack of cigarettes.

"*You* stole my money!" he cried.

"Listen, here, young feller," said the man, as his blue eyes turned to steel gray.

"We don't think much of a man who falls off a steamboat in a calm sea. Maybe you cracked your head on something when you fell, or you surely wouldn't be standing here on my boat, the *We're Here*, telling me, Captain Disko Troop, that me and my crew is a pack of thieves."

"But you are!" said Harvey.

"Think what you like," said Disko Troop. "But we just got out here on the Banks, and we can't afford to go home until we fill our hold with fish. So here's my offer. You do your share of the work with Dan, and I'll pay you $10.50 every month until we get back to the port of Gloucester in September."

"But this is only May!" Harvey yelled. "I can't stay here and fish for four months! Take me to New York at once! I demand it! Name your price, you thief!"

Wham!

The next time Harvey woke up, he was lying on the deck with a nose full of blood.

Chapter Two

Pitching Fish

"You had that bloody nose coming to you," said Dan, "and I know just how you feel. Dad laid me out once, and that was enough for me!"

"But I didn't deserve it!" Harvey sobbed, as he mopped the blood from his face. "That man's either crazy or drunk!"

"Don't let him hear you say that," said Dan. "He's dead set against liquor and he thinks *you're* crazy for saying your father is a millionaire!"

"A multi-millionaire!" Harvey corrected. "He owns gold mines out West!"

"Does he ride a pony and shoot pistols, too?"

"If my father wants to ride somewhere, he takes his car. Have you even seen a car, Dan?"

"I seen one once."

"Well, my father owns two cars and a private railroad car besides," said Harvey.

"You're lyin'," said Dan. "Let me hear you swear, 'I hope I may die if I ain't speaking the truth.' " To Dan's way of thinking, this was the most terrible oath a boy could utter.

"Hope I may die right here," said Harvey, "if every word I've spoken isn't the cold truth."

Then Dan asked Harvey every question he could think of about the private railroad and Harvey had an answer for every one.

Not only that, but Harvey had sworn an oath and he was still alive, so Dan figured he must be telling the truth.

"Gosh!" said Dan at last, "Dad's made a mistake for once in his life!"

"Yes," said Harvey, "and I'll get even with him for robbing me!"

"Now hold on," said Dan. "Manuel fished you out of the ocean and me and Dad helped pull you onto the *We're Here*. Wherever your money went, *we* didn't steal it. And that goes for the rest of the crew as well."

"I guess for somebody who just got saved from drowning, I don't sound too grateful," Harvey admitted. By now the bleeding had stopped, and he was thinking more clearly. Harvey stood up and wobbled back to where Captain Disko Troop was sitting. Harvey took a deep breath and said, "I'm here to take back those things I said. When a man is saved from drowning, he shouldn't go off calling people names. I'm here to say I'm sorry."

"Young feller, that's right," said Disko. He reached out his eleven-inch hand and squeezed Harvey's hand until he felt numb to his elbow. "Now you and Dan go on about your work."

Up on deck, Dan smiled and said, "You did the right thing, Harvey. My dad's a fair man, and he's *always* right."

* * *

It was evening. The boys watched as half a dozen small dories rowed back to the *We're Here*.

"Here comes Manuel, the man who saved you," said Dan. "Come on, there's work to do!"

"But I've never done work," said Harvey, embarrassed.

"Just do what I say. Grab on to that block and tackle behind you."

"Block and tackle?"

"The rope hanging from that pulley," explained Dan. "Grab the long iron hook on that rope."

As Manuel's dory came alongside, the boys handed him two iron hooks, which he attached to the ends of his boat.

"Is good catch!" Manuel yelled in his Portuguese accent as he climbed aboard the *We're Here*. "Two hundred and thirty-one! Hey, new boy! You pretty well now? Last night the fish, they fish for you. Now you fish for fish! Eh? Dan, you got time to clean out my boat?"

"Glad to do it, Manuel," came Dan's reply.

Harvey felt he should pay Manuel, but then he remembered about his money, and then he heard Dan's call.

"Pull!" Dan shouted.

Harvey pulled on his rope and was amazed to see Manuel's dory rise up from the water and onto the deck.

"Ready for the next one, Harve?" called Dan. "It's Long Jack, the Irishman from Galway. Them Galway men are good in a boat!"

Soon the boys were raising Irish Long Jack's dory and placing it on top of Manuel's like a stack of dishes.

"One hundred and forty-nine and a half!" said Long Jack, scratching his whiskered chin. "Bad catch today! The Portugee has beat me!"

"Harvey, see this next man rowing in?" said Dan. "That's old Tom Platt. See that scar across his face? He got it on the man-o'-war *Ohio*, fighting in the Civil War. But don't ask him about it or he'll be talking about the war all night!"

"Two hundred and three!" bellowed old Tom Platt.

He climbed up on deck and watched as Harvey pulled up the footboards in the dory and wiped away the fish slime.

"He's caught on good," said Tom.

The last two dories came alongside. In one dory was a skinny little man called Penn, short for Pennsylvania. In the other dory was Dan's Uncle Salters. Neither of them seemed able to count.

"I think it's 42," Penn called in a small voice.

"Well I caught 45!" said Uncle Salters.

"No, *I* caught 45," said Penn.

"But you just said 42! Count again, you old farmer!"

"This beats the circus any day," said Dan.

Everyone on board roared with laughter.

"Seat ye!" called a new voice from the cabin. It was the cook, a huge, jet-black Negro named MacDonald calling the men to dinner. MacDonald was from Cape Breton in Canada, where his family had fled during the Civil War.

Harvey was about to go in when Dan held him back. Harvey watched hungrily as Tom, Long Jack, Uncle Salters, and Disko Troop all headed forward to eat.

"See, Harvey," said Dan, "the cook can't feed everyone at the same time, so the oldest men eat first."

Harvey was starving by the time the second half of the men got to eat.

MacDonald gave them hot bread, strong coffee and made a stew with scraps of pork, fried potatoes and fish tongues. The coffee was the strongest that Harvey had ever tasted.

* * *

In the moonlight after supper, the work of cutting, cleaning, and salting the hundreds of fish began. Dan had set up tables beside a heaping pen filled with dead fish.

Manuel and Penn stood knee-deep in the fish. Manuel picked one up.

With the flash of a knife, he slit it from
head to tail and passed it on to Irish Long
Jack. Jack scooped out the fish's liver and
dropped it in a basket. He tore off the
fish's head and threw the head away with
the guts. Then he slid the fish down
along a table to Uncle Salters, who cut out
the backbone and dropped the fish meat in
a tub.

Harvey's job was to scoop up the fish
with a pitchfork and throw it down into
the hold, where Uncle Salters, Disko, and
Dan were packing the fish in salt.

At the end of an hour, Harvey's back
was aching, and he would have given
the world to rest, but he was proud to be
working with the men.

After two hours he was practically
dead.

"At last *rest!*" he thought when the last
fish was salted away and the old men had
gone off to their bunks.

"Hold on, Harvey. You and me get to clean up this mess," yelled Dan, pointing at the slime and fish guts that littered the tables and deck.

For another hour, the two of them scrubbed and cleaned.

"Now can I sleep?" Harvey begged.

"No, we're on the first night watch!" Dan growled.

"But why?"

"In case some fool steamship tries to run us down!"

"But I can't!"

"You can!" Dan yelled. He picked up a short rope and cracked it like a whip. "And I'll beat you if you fall asleep!"

Chapter Three

Beginner's Luck

Next morning, the boys cleaned the plates and pans from breakfast, then went up on deck. Harvey filled his lungs with the sweet, salt air. The sky was clear. The day was quiet. All around the *We're Here*, other schooners were now anchored, and dozens of dories were fishing.

"Where did all those other boats come from?" Harvey asked Dan.

"They sneaked up on us during the night," Dan replied. "See Dad standing over there by the cabin, just smoking his pipe? Pretty soon we'll move, and all those other captains out there are just waiting to see where we go. They know that Dad's the best there is at thinking like a fish."

"Thinking like a fish?"

"Yeah, figuring out where to find the most fish. The Grand Banks is a lot of open sea. Some men spend a lifetime trying to guess where the fish might be. Nobody does it better than Disko Troop. He studies the weather, the currents, what the fish might be eating, and a million other things. See over there? That boat is the *Carrie Pitman*. She'd just drift all over the Banks if she didn't have the *We're Here* to follow. But Dad will give 'em the slip!"

Dan called to his father. "Dad, we've done our chores. Can we go out?"

"You can go," said Disko, "but not until you get Harvey out of that cherry-colored suit of his! Give him some proper clothes."

Dan gave Harvey his extra set of clothes and boots. Then they climbed down into Dan's own dory, the *Hattie S.*, and pushed off. Harvey had never rowed a boat on an ocean, and he was amazed at the power of the waves. The water seemed to tug at the oars. *Crack!* An oar handle smacked Harvey in the jaw. After that, he held on tighter but his hands began to blister.

"Let's try here," said Dan. He took an oar and held it straight up in the air. A mile away in another dory, Manuel raised his arm three times.

"Manuel says it's 30 fathoms deep around here," said Dan.

"How deep is that in feet?" asked Harvey.

"Well, one fathom's the same as six feet."

Harvey was quick with numbers. "So it's 180 feet deep here," he said.

"I guess," said Dan, as he picked up a reel of fishing line and baited the hook with a clam. "Do like me, Harvey, and don't get your line all tangled," he said, tossing the line over the side.

Harvey was still trying to bait his own hook when Dan shouted, "Here we come!" A burst of spray shot up from the water as a big cod flapped alongside. "Muckle, Harvey, muckle!" yelled Dan. "Under your hand! Quick!"

A wooden hammer lay by Harvey's feet. Harvey handed it to Dan. *Whack!* Dan stunned the fish with a single blow and began to haul it in.

Suddenly, Harvey felt a tug on his line and pulled up. "Hey, look!!" he shouted. "Strawberries!" He reached out to grab them.

"Don't touch them!" Dan warned, but the warning came too late.

"Ouch!" cried Harvey. His hand felt as though it had grabbed a fistful of needles. "What are these things?"

"Not strawberries, that's for sure!" said Dan. "They're jellyfish, and they sting like sin!"

"*Now* you tell me!" said Harvey, rubbing his hand on the side of the boat.

"Dad says naked fingers should only touch fish. Next time you get a jellyfish, scrape it off."

Harvey thought about what his nervous mother would be saying if she saw him there. Just as the pain eased off, Harvey's line suddenly peeled out through his fingers.

"Let me help," said Dan.

"No!" yelled Harvey. "It's my first fish and it feels like a whale!"

Dan peered over the side. Something big and white was moving around below the dory. "Halibut! And he's over a hundred! I better help you, Harve."

"No!"

Harvey's knuckles were raw and bleeding as he banged them against the gunwale, straining to bring up the fish. After 20 minutes of struggle, he finally pulled the fish to the surface.

"Muckle!" shouted Harvey.

Whack!

They pulled the halibut over the rail and into the dory.

"It's all of a hundred," Dan said.

Harvey's body ached all over as he looked with pride at his huge fish.

* * *

"Stow these fish in a hurry!" Disko ordered, when the boys returned to the ship. The rest of the crew was also back from fishing. "Boys, it's time we looked for better fishing. As soon as the weather changes, we sail."

Harvey looked around. He couldn't see any sign of a change. The sky was blue, and there wasn't a cloud in sight.

Dan grinned and gave him a nudge. "Dad reads the sky like he reads the sea. Just wait," he muttered, "you'll see."

Amazingly, a short while later, a fog rose up around them and the wind began to blow. Long Jack and Uncle Salters pulled up the anchor.

"Up jib-sail and foresail," commanded Disko, standing at the wheel.

The *We're Here* began to move through the fog. In a calm, steady voice, Disko gave orders to raise more sails. Soon, waves were breaking hard against the bow.

"What do we do now?" Harvey asked Dan.

"Nothing much," said Dan. "Just wait to get to where we're going."

"Need something to do?" said Long Jack. "Maybe it's time for Harvey to learn the ropes!"

With that, Long Jack began to march Harvey up and down the deck, holding him by the back of the neck.

"Now *that's* the front of the boat," he said, marching toward the bow. "But we don't call it 'the front of the boat.' We call it the *bow*. What do we call it?"

"Bow!" Harvey echoed, as Long Jack's fingers pinched.

Then Long Jack spun him around. "And that's the back of the boat and we call it the *stern*. What do we call it?"

"Stern!"

"And the right side of the ship is *starboard*, and the left is *port*!"

"Starboard! Port!" Harvey yelled in pain.

"And our big mast is called the *main-mast*, see?"

"Main-mast!"

Up and down, Long Jack marched Harvey until the boy's head ached with names. Whenever Harvey forgot and got one wrong, Long Jack would lash him with the end of a rope until he got it right. The lashes hurt, but when Harvey looked angry, the lashes only got harder. This was learn or else!

Chapter Four

Jonahs
and Floods

When Harvey awoke the next morning,
the schooner was plowing through heavy
seas, waves spraying across the deck as
the *We're Here* rolled this way and that.
The whole schooner seemed to sing with
the wind in its sails. Harvey was pleased
with himself that he was not deathly sick
from the rolling.

The men passed the time in their usual
ways. Uncle Salters and Penn played

checkers. MacDonald peeled potatoes. Tom Platt told again a story about a sea battle in the Civil War. Dan wrestled with an accordion in the cramped quarters and began to play some tunes.

Manuel looked over at Harvey.

"You lucky to be alive, you know," Manuel said. "If I was you, when I come to Gloucester, I go to the church and light candles to the Blessed Virgin. She put you in my boat and saved you. She very good to fishermen. That is why so few Portuguese men ever drown."

"Oh, that's all just superstition," said Tom Platt, lying back in his bunk. "The sea does what it wants. It don't care how many candles you light. Come on, Dan, sing us another song."

Dan began to sing and play, but he had just begun when old Tom sat up.

"Hold on!" Tom roared. "Do you want to ruin the whole trip with that song, Dan? That song is a Jonah if anyone sings it before we're heading home!"

"Ain't no such thing," said Dan.
"You can't learn me anything about Jonahs.
If you don't like it, Tom, get out your fiddle
and we'll sing something else."

Harvey watched as Tom unwrapped
an old white fiddle. Manuel took out
a tiny guitar-like thing. His eyes caught
Harvey's. "A Portuguese guitar," said
Manuel. "It's called a *nachette*."

"What's a Jonah?" Harvey asked Tom.

"Jonah was a man in the Bible who
brought bad luck wherever he sailed," said
Tom, "so a Jonah is anything that spoils
the luck of men at sea. Sometimes it's
a dory, and sometimes it's a man. There's
all sorts of Jonahs. A boy could be a
Jonah," he said, looking straight at Harvey.

"Now how can you believe *that*
superstition if you don't believe in lighting
candles to the Virgin?" asked Harvey.

"Don't go makin' fun of Jonahs, young
fellow," Disko said.

"Harve ain't no Jonah!" said Dan.

"Didn't we catch plenty of fish the very day after we pulled him in?"

MacDonald the cook threw back his head and let out a chilling laugh. "Oh, yes!" he agreed, "but the catch is not finished yet. Big fish catch little fish. One day Harvey will be your master, Danny."

"Now that's news," Dan said with a laugh.

"Master!" said the cook, pointing to Harvey. "Man!" and he pointed to Dan.

"It's Dan that's going to be the master of this ship one day," said Tom Platt, "if he don't get drowned in the meantime. Where in thunder did you get that fool idea, MacDonald?"

"I do not know," MacDonald answered softly, "but so it will be. Master and man." Then he went back to peeling potatoes.

"Well," said Dan, "it don't look to me like Harvey could ever be *my* master, but at least he ain't no Jonah. If anyone on this boat is a Jonah, it's Uncle Salters. He sure

never catches much! He ought to be on
the *Carrie Pitman*. That's the boat where
Jonahs belong. She can't even make her
own anchor stick to the floor of the sea!"

* * *

The wind was still strong and the
waves were enormous, but the sky had
cleared, and things were drier up on deck.
The boys went up to look around. They
found Penn and Uncle Salters already there,
together at the wheel.

"What's wrong with Penn?" asked
Harvey. "He looks so sad all the time,
and he follows your uncle around like
a lost dog."

"He's lost his mind, I guess you'd say,"
said Dan, "ever since his wife and four
kids drowned."

"Drowned?"

"And on dry land, too! I mean it!"
said Dan. "One night about five years ago,
they was staying in a river town in
Pennsylvania called Johnstown.

There used to be a big dam on that river way above the town. Well, one day the dam breaks and all that water comes rushing down and sweeps the town away, along with Penn's wife and their four little kids."

"Penn's real name is Jacob Boller," Dan continued, "but most of the time he can't remember who he is. He used to be a preacher, too. But don't ever say nothin' out loud about this, or he might remember his dead wife and kids and maybe try to kill himself!"

"How did Penn and Uncle Salters get together?" asked Harvey.

"Uncle Salters had a farm and he took Penn in. Been looking after him ever since. When Uncle Salters sold the farm, Dad let them come fishing on the *We're Here*."

A sad thought came into Harvey's mind. He wondered how *his* mother must be feeling right now, thinking that her only child was drowned at sea. He wondered whether his father had even received the news.

Chapter Five

Ways of the Sea

Uncle Salters pointed at the wild waves and said, "Seems to me I saw a boat over yonder."

"It can't be one of ours," said Disko. He turned to Dan and said, "Son, climb up the rigging and have a look."

Harvey marveled at how quickly Dan could climb the rope ladder while the boat pitched this way and that on the rough sea.

"It's the Captain Abishai's boat," yelled Dan, "and she's in trouble, sure!"

Salters groaned. Every man on the *We're Here* hated Captain Abishai. In fact, they hated everything about him: his boat, his crew, and his cheating, drunken ways.

"He's the worst kind of Jonah," said Long Jack. "Look how he's running her in this weather. He'll have her sunk in no time."

Abishai's boat was now close enough for Harvey to see what Long Jack meant. The boat was pitching into the waves. Its ropes and rigging were a tangled mess. Its men were hanging on for dear life.

The gray-bearded captain yelled across to Disko. "You'll not survive *this* gale!" he warned. "You'll not reach port again!"

"You crazy fool," muttered Disko.

The men on the *We're Here* watched the Abishai's ship roll over a wave, then slide down the other side and out of view. The boat did not rise up on the next swell.

"Glory be!" said Long Jack, "she's sunk!"

"Drunk or sober, we've got to help them!" shouted Disko.

The men pulled up anchor, and Disko turned the *We're Here* to where Abishai's boat had vanished. But all that remained was an empty bottle of gin and two or three wooden tubs bobbing in the water.

Harvey could not believe that he had just seen death on the open waters. He suddenly felt very sick.

"Let that be a lesson, boy," said Disko. "A boat can sink mighty quick hereabouts. But *that* boat sank on account of liquor."

* * *

As the days passed, Harvey was accepted more and more among the crew as a boy to be trained in the ways of the sea. He was eager to learn all he could. Since he had not grown up at sea, he could never be as good as Dan at the hands-on work.

And Dan could always beat him in a fight.
Dan also had something else that Harvey
envied: a girlfriend named Hattie B. But
Harvey was a quick thinker and good with
numbers. Soon Disko was teaching him
how to use the sun and stars to figure out
where they were on Disko's maps of the sea.

Disko taught Harvey how to use a tool
called a quadrant to
read the angle of the
sun. Each day,
precisely at noon, they
would use the quadrant
to measure how high
the sun was in the sky.
That angle would tell
them their latitude, which is how far
north or south they were from the equator.
Once they knew their latitude, they only
needed to figure out how far east or west
they were. This was called their longitude.
Once they knew both latitude and
longitude, they would know where they
were on the maps.

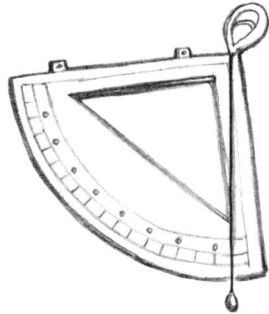

One way that Disko could figure out

the longitude was by checking the angles
of certain stars at certain times of night.
Another way was to measure the depth
of the water. To do this, Harvey would
take a sounding. A sounding meant taking
a long rope with a weight on the end and
tossing it over the side to see how deep
it went. The rope had marks on it for every
fathom. Disko knew how many fathoms
deep the water was at different places on
his maps.

The surprising thing to Harvey was
how many other boats did not know where
they were or where they were going! One
foggy day, the *We're Here* crossed the path
of a cattle boat that was trying to cross
the ocean to Europe. In the fog, its captain
had no idea where he was, so he called out
to Disko to beg for directions.

Old Uncle Salters, the farmer, was
thrilled. He started to give the lost captain
advice about what to feed cattle, while
everyone else on the *We're Here* held
their noses. That old cow-boat stank like
a hundred tons of wet manure.

Disko got angry at Salters. "We're fishermen, not farmers!" he grumbled. "The whole fishing fleet will be laughing at us when they find out you've been giving advice about feeding cows!"

* * *

When the fog was bad, Harvey might spend the whole day ringing a bell on the schooner so that the men out fishing in the dories would be able to find their way back to the ship. Once in a while, when days were clear and the wind was light, Disko taught Harvey how to steer the schooner from one good fishing spot to another.

"It's beautiful how quick he learns," said Long Jack one day as he watched Harvey using the quadrant. "Hey, Disko, look how well the boy is doing. You sure were wrong for once, when you called him crazy and cracked in the head!"

"He *was* crazy!" Disko replied. "But I cured him."

"Well, he still tells some crazy yarns," said Tom Platt.

"Last night he told us about some rich kid that owned four ponies. He says he knows kids that get birthday presents of solid silver! What a fairy-tale that was, I reckon!"

"I guess he makes 'em up," said Disko. "Dan is the only fool who believes them stories. And I'm not even sure *he* does."

The crew never worked on Sundays. Instead, they told stories or rested. Or else Penn sang hymns or read the Bible aloud. But if Penn ever started to preach, Salters would stop him.

"But Penn *is* a preacher!" Harvey told Dan behind the men's backs.

"I know," said Dan. "But Uncle Salters doesn't want him to remember his old life. Then he might remember the Johnstown flood, and we all know where that could lead!"

All the crewmen were good to the boys, but MacDonald the cook paid them special attention. And he never took back his

prediction that one day Harvey would be
Dan's master. At mealtime he would
always ask Harvey, and Harvey alone, if
he liked the food. Of course, that made
everyone laugh, because to them, Harvey
was nothing more than a boy with a great
deal left to learn.

* * *

The *We're Here* moved from spot to
spot around the Banks, steadily filling its
hold with salted fish. Sometimes, other
boats caught up with it and fished nearby.
But Disko would always slip away and
look for places for his men to fish alone.
He didn't like crowds. He didn't like men
who followed in a herd like sheep.

"But there's one place where we'll have
to put up with all those other boats," he told
Harvey one day. He pointed to a shallow
spot on the charts that was called the Old
Virgin. "Pretty soon, the time will be right
for fishing close around the skirts of the
Old Virgin. They'll be so many boats there
that it's like a roaring town on the water."

Chapter Six

The Bad News
Carrie Pitman

"Squid ho!" Uncle Salters yelled one night when he was on watch.

Everyone ran up on deck. A squid is the best kind of bait there is for catching cod, and a squid is easy to catch. All you have to do is lower a small red ball of lead into the water.

For some mysterious reason, a squid will wrap its tentacles around the ball of lead and let itself be pulled out of the sea before it lets go. Harvey discovered soon enough why each man seemed to dance around and jerk his head from side to side as he pulled a squid over the rail. As each squid passed near the man's face, it shot a stream of water, then a stream of ink at its captor. When the squid catch was finished, the crew looked as if they had been sprayed with black paint.

The next day, the *Carrie Pitman* sailed right up close to the *We're Here*. The *Carrie Pitman* could never set its anchor right, so it was always drifting into other fishing boats in the middle of the night. Dan shouted across the water and boasted about the squid they had just caught.

"We'll trade you seven cod for one squid," yelled the captain of the *Pitman*.

"No deal," answered Disko. "And don't be dropping anchor near here. You'll tangle our anchor for sure."

The *Pitman* drifted about a half a mile away, put down its anchor and tried to catch some squid. Disko told Dan and Manuel to attach a marker called a buoy to their own anchor.

"Why?" asked Harvey.

"Because if the *Carrie Pitman* loses her anchor tonight, she'll drift into us in the dark," Dan replied. "If that happens, we'll have to cut our own anchor line to get out of the way before we get wrecked. If we don't tie a buoy to the line, we'll never find our anchor again."

That night, Dan and Harvey were on watch. And sure enough, suddenly the *Carrie Pitman* came drifting right toward their ship.

"Glory, hallelujah!" Dan yelled. "Here she comes, butt-first! Dad, she's walkin' in her sleep again!"

In an instant Disko ran up on deck and cut the anchor line with an ax. Then he steered the *We're Here* just barely out of way of the *Carrie Pitman*.

"Good evening, Jonah!" Disko shouted angrily as it passed. "And how does your garden grow?"

"You're not fishermen, you're farmers," continued Uncle Salters. "You don't need sails, you need a mule! Go back to Ohio!"

The rest of the crew of the *We're Here* joined in, each shouting something a little nastier than the one before.

* * *

But the *Carrie Pitman* wasn't the only Jonah. The next night, a little before dawn, the sea was lost in a milky fog. Harvey and Dan were up on deck taking turns at ringing the bell to warn other boats away. Suddenly they heard the shrieking siren of an ocean liner charging through the fog.

"*Aoooooooo!*" went the steamship's siren.

"*Tinkle—tink!*" went the bell on the *We're Here*.

"They must be going 20 miles an hour," Dan said angrily. "And they hardly even slow down when they hit us!"

Harvey felt sick and ashamed as he listened to Dan's words. He remembered his last night as a passenger on one of those liners, when he had wished that they would run over a fishing boat.

A moment later, the great bow of the liner loomed up out of the fog like a steel cliff. A row of gleaming portholes sailed by as the giant steamship hissed past. The *We're Here* staggered and shook in the swirl of the steamship's huge propellers. Harvey felt sick as he heard a cracking sound as the stern of the liner vanished in the fog.

In the distance, a voice called, "You've sunk us!"

"Is it *us*?" gasped Harvey.

"No!" Dan yelled. "It's a boat out yonder. Lower the dories! We're going out to look. Keep ringing the bell, Harvey!"

No sooner had Dan and the others disappeared into the fog, than a broken mast of a fishing schooner drifted by, followed by an empty dory. Then followed something, facedown, in a blue sweater, but — Harvey could see that it was only half of a man.

"It was the *Jennie Cushman*," Dan wailed as he pulled his dory alongside. "That steamship cut her clean in half. Its propellers ground her up like chopped meat!"

A short while later, Disko brought in the other dory with Jason Olley, the *Jennie Cushman*'s gray-haired captain.

"Disko, what did you pick me up for?" he groaned. "I've lost the crew, I've lost my son, I've lost everything!"

Disko only laid a hand on the poor man's shoulder.

Suddenly Penn came up to him. Harvey could see that something was different about Penn.

He was standing straight and tall, and his foolish face seemed suddenly wise. In a strong voice he declared, "The Lord gave, and the Lord has taken away. Blessed be the name of the Lord! I was — I *am* a minister of the Lord. Leave this man to me."

"Oh, you're a preacher, are you?" said poor old Olley. "Then pray my son back to me! Pray back my $9,000 boat and my thousands of pounds of fish! And *you* be the one to tell my wife that her son is dead!"

"Go below and lie down, Jason Olley," said Disko sadly. "There ain't nothin' more to say."

Penn and the old man stared into each other's eyes. "Come below with me, old man!" he ordered, and he led Jason Olley down into the cabin.

"That ain't Penn," cried Uncle Salters.

"That's old Jacob Boller, the preacher!   Next thing, he's going to remember Johnstown and *his* family that drowned there.   What am I going to do now?"

A while later, Penn came back up on deck alone.

"I have prayed," he said.   "My own wife and children were drowned before my eyes, and I never was able to pray for their lives, but now I have prayed for this man's son, and he will surely be sent back to him." Then he looked straight at Uncle Salters and asked, "How long have I been mad?"

"Oh, you weren't never *mad*," Salters lied.

"About five years," said Disko.

"And have I been a burden to you all this time?" asked Penn.

"No!" cried Uncle Salters twisting his hands together.   "You ain't never was a burden to no one!"

Penn looked around at the other men's faces. "You are good men," he said. "Please tell me the—"

Just then the bell of another schooner rang nearby, and a voice called through the fog. "Disko Troop! Did ya' hear about the *Jennie Cushman*?"

"This boat has found Jason Olley's son. I'm sure of it!" cried Penn. "The boy has been saved by the Lord!"

The crew of the *We're Here* stared out into the fog as the other boat came in view. It was the *Carrie Pitman*.

"We got Jason Olley aboard here," Disko called out to the crew of the *Pitman*. "But there weren't anyone else alive."

"We found one," said the voice from the *Pitman*. "To tell you the truth, we was just driftin' when we come across him, hanging onto some broken lumber."

"Who is he?"

"I suppose it's young Olley.   He says he's the captain's son."

"Praise God!" Penn cried and raised his hands.

A short while later, old Jason Olley was rowed over to the *Pitman* to join his son.

"And now—," said Penn, looking at Uncle Salters.   "And now—."

The crew watched as the tall straight body and voice of Jacob Boller sank back into the familiar man everyone called Penn. His body went slack again and the bright light faded from his eyes.

"And now, Mr. Salters," said Penn, "I think it's time for a game of checkers."

Chapter Seven

In Town

"Boys, we're in town!" Disko yelled down to the crew in the cabin below.

Harvey was the first on deck. To the end of his days, he would never forget the sight. After almost a week of fog, the sun was rising on a clear, blue horizon. Its red rays struck the masts of a hundred schooners at anchor, bobbing on the open sea. From every schooner, dories were dropping away like bees from a hive.

Across the water Harvey heard the splashing of dozens of oars and the excited voices of a thousand fishermen.

"Disko was right," said Harvey. "It *is* like a town!"

"And over yonder is the Virgin," said Disko, pointing to a patch of greenish sea where there were no dories. The "Virgin" was the name of a large flat area of hidden rock that sat like a big shelf about four or five fathoms below the surface of the water. It was dangerous to fish in this patch of sea because at any time the waves might be suddenly sucked away, sending the fishing boats crashing against the bare rock. The codfish had now gathered all around the edges of this dangerous rock by the thousands, and the entire fleet had gathered there to haul them in.

"Fish everywhere you can," Disko told his crew, "but stay away from the Virgin."

Harvey and Dan went out. It was wonderful fishing.

The boys could see glimmering cod swimming everywhere. Dories were crowded all around them, and the men called to one another with jokes and gossip.

"Say, Tom Platt! Over there, is that the boy you all picked up off a steamboat? How's the little sea-puppy doing? Is he worth his salt yet?"

"He's an old sea-dog now, I'll have you know! He's worth his salt and more!"

"Oh, is he? I don't see much hair on his chin!"

"He's working on it! One day, he'll grow better seaweed than you!"

"Ha! Ha!"

The schooners rocked and dipped, like mother ducks watching their ducklings. Pretty soon, the dories were banging into each other, fighting for the best spots to fish. Fishing lines and anchor lines got tangled, and angry men swore back and forth.

It was a wild fishing ground, but cod and fishermen were not the only wild things in it. Now and then, a playful whale would snag an anchor line and pull the dory for a half a mile before the whale would shake itself loose.

Every night meant another huge pile of fish on deck, a pile so big that Dan and Harvey would fall asleep in the middle of pitching and salting them down.

Harvey found out soon enough why no dory dared to fish too near the Virgin. One day he watched as two crazy Irishmen rowed their dory over the top of the rock and dropped anchor there. Some fishermen yelled at them to come away, while others dared them to stay. Long Jack rowed after them, and when he reached them, he pulled out his knife and cut their anchor line.

Then he stood up in his dory and yelled, "Can't you hear the Virgin's warning? Get away and row for your miserable lives!"

The men in the dory swore at Long Jack as he rowed away. Then suddenly, the sea gave a heave and a couple of acres of foaming water shot straight up from the shelf of rock, leaving it bare. The Irishmen barely escaped with their lives.

"Ain't it beautiful?" said Dan. "Watch now, Harvey. The Virgin will break out of the water about once every 15 minutes. She'll do that as regular as a clock for a while, and she'll bash out the bottom of any dory that tries to fish above her! You've seen the greatest thing on the Banks, and if it wasn't for Long Jack, you'd have seen dead men, too!"

But they would see more dead men soon enough, for all that night the Virgin roared. Next morning, all around, the sea was crowned with angry waves.

"No fishing today," Disko ordered his crew.

But other schooners did send out their dories.

That evening, the crew of the *We're Here*
stood with lanterns, hauling wet fishermen
out of the terrible sweeping waves. Lost
dories pitched themselves against the side
of the ship and were smashed to pieces.

The next morning, Harvey counted
seven extra mouths at breakfast. The whole
fleet spent the day sorting things out and
getting lost men back to the schooners
where they belonged. Four men had
drowned. One of them was from a
French-Canadian schooner from Quebec.
The dead man's schooner sailed off by itself
to a patch of deep water to give the man
a funeral. As Harvey watched through
Disko's spyglass, a large bundle was thrown
over the side of the ship. It was a body
wrapped in rope and canvas.

That night the sea was black and
peppered with the reflection of stars.
Across the water came a slow, sad hymn
from the crew of the French schooner,
bidding their comrade good-bye.

Chapter Eight

Dead Man's Revenge

Two boats from Gloucester were ahead of all the others in catching their full loads of fish. One was the *Parry Norman*, and the other was the *We're Here*. The first boat to fill its hold with salted cod would also be first to sail back to port. To be first in port was a special honor, so day after day both crews fished hard.

News had spread that the French boat was holding an auction to sell the clothes and property of the dead man. Dan and Harvey took a break from fishing and join the other dories that had gone to the auction.

The dead man's property was spread out on the roof of the cabin: a red cap, a pair of boots, a leather belt with a knife that had a brass handle. Dan bought the belt with the knife. By the time he and Harvey dropped the *Hattie S.* back into the water, a drizzle of rain began to fall. A short while later, they were rowing through a heavy fog.

"Heave over the anchor, Harve," said Dan. "Let's fish a while until this fog lifts."

The fog was thick and cold. The current tugged the bow of the dory hard against the anchor line. Harvey turned up his collar around his neck and hunched over his reel to bait a hook. For a while, they fished in silence. Then Dan drew the knife out of its sheath and tested its blade on the rail.

"That's a daisy of a knife," said Harvey. "How did you get it so cheap?"

"On account of them being so superstitious. They think it's bad luck to take a knife off a dead man."

"But someone took his boots," said Harvey.

"Boots is different," said Dan. "Besides, one of the Frenchmen told me that this knife was used to kill a man last year. When I heard *that*, I wanted it even more!"

"Christmas! I didn't know about a murder!" said Harvey. "I'll give you a dollar for it when I — get my wages. Say, I'll give you two dollars!"

"Honest? Do you like it that much?" said Dan. "To tell the truth, I bought it to give to you. It's yours because we're dory mates."

He held out the belt and knife to Harvey.

Harvey couldn't believe it. "Dan, you're a man," he said. "I'll keep it as long as I live!"

Dan grinned and turned back to his reel as Harvey put on the belt.

They both went back to fishing. Harvey began to tug on his line.

"Darn the thing!" he said. "She acts like she's stuck on the bottom but it's all sand here."

"Could be a big halibut," Dan replied. "Here, let me help you."

The two boys pulled together, and slowly the heavy thing began to move up.

"Here she comes!" Dan shouted, but the shout ended in a shrill cry of horror. —"Aaaaa!"

Out of the sea came the body of the Frenchman who had been buried two days before. The hook had caught him under the armpit, and now his head and shoulders

were swaying above the water. His arms
had been tied to his sides, and — he had
no face. The boys fell over each other in a
heap at the bottom of the dory, screaming
while the thing bobbed alongside, held fast
by the fishing line.

"The tide — the tide must have brought
him!" stammered Harvey.

"Oh, Lord!" groaned Dan. "He's come
for it, Harve! Let him have it!"

"Have what?"

"His knife! Quick! Take it off!"

"*I* don't want it!" cried Harvey, as he
struggled with the belt buckle!

"Faster, Harve! He's on *your* line!"

Harvey sat up, took out the knife,
and cut the line. The body shot down with
a plop. Harvey flung the belt and knife out
as far as he could throw. Dan rose to his
knees. His face was whiter than the fog.

"Oh, Harve! Did you see his face? He come for it special! He was looking just for us!"

"Look here, Dan," said Harvey. "It was only the tide. He never meant nothing."

"Tide? No, he come for it. They sunk him six miles from here and weighed him down with nine feet of chain. Say — what are you doing with your fish?"

"Throwing them overboard," said Harvey.

"What for? *We* won't be eating them."

"Don't you know what those fish were eating?" asked Harvey. "Didn't you see? That Frenchman had no face left!"

Dan said nothing and began throwing his fish over the side.

For an hour or more they sat there shivering in the empty boat, wondering what other evil things were hiding out there in the fog.

"I'd give a month's pay if this fog would lift so we could see where we are," said Dan.

Then a strange, muffled voice came across the water. "Oooh, Danny! Oooh, Haarvee?"

"It's him again!" yelled Dan.

"Hold on, it's the cook, MacDonald!" said Harvey. "Hello, MacDonald! Over here!"

A few moments later, MacDonald rowed out of the fog.

"Oh, boys! What happened?" asked MacDonald. "Captain Disko will beat you blue for fooling around out here like this!"

"Please! It's all right if he beats us!" cried Dan. "Just get us back to the boat!"

* * *

The *We're Here* raced neck and neck with the *Parry Norman* to be the first boat heading home. Every day, as the two crews fished and cut and salted from dawn until late at night, the rest of the fleet made bets on which boat would win.

One morning, Disko hauled out the mainsail. By noon, all the sails on the *We're Here* were up, and its flag was flying to tell the rest of the fleet that the *We're Here* would be the first to go home. On deck, Dan pumped his accordion and Tom Platt sawed on his fiddle as the schooner proudly toured the fleet to pick up everyone's mail before turning its bow toward Gloucester harbor.

Chapter Nine

A Captain Rolls East

On a gray September morning, the
We're Here sailed into Gloucester harbor.
As it docked at the wharf, its flag was
at half-mast for Otto, the young Dutch
man of the crew who had drowned at sea
a month before Harvey had been saved.
Otto had been planning to be married when
he returned to Gloucester.

A tall woman stepped down into the schooner and kissed Dan once upon the cheek. It was Dan's mother.

Suddenly, Harvey felt like the loneliest boy in the world. He sat by the wheel and sobbed.

Mrs. Troop led Disko, Dan and Harvey home to hot baths, the smells of dinner, and warm, new nightshirts. The next day, Harvey sent a telegram to San Diego, California, and received a reply which he secretly shared with Dan.

That night, Dan teased his father. "Harve's folks don't amount to much after all, Dad," he said. "You'll get paid five dollars if you're lucky."

* * *

Out in his office in San Diego, Harvey Cheyne Senior had been trying hard not to give up. He was an important businessman, and at that moment his secretary, Mr. Milsom, was asking him about a problem in one of Cheyne's lumber mills.

But what did Mr. Cheyne care? He had no heart to crush his enemies in the great money battles any more. What was the point of going on, now that his only son had been lost at sea? And all the doctors in the world couldn't cure the broken heart of the boy's poor mother, Constance Cheyne.

But Mr. Cheyne was tough. He gave Mr. Milsom some reply and slouched behind his desk, thinking, *if only I'd spent more time with my son, instead of waiting for the boy to grow up! I always dreamed of the day when all my millions would be his, and now?*

He stared at his boots.

"Sir?" Mr. Milsom placed a telegram in Cheyne's hands. The words all ran together, and Cheyne had to read them slowly:

PICKED UP BY FISHING SCHOONER WE'RE HERE AFTER FALLING OFF BOAT GREAT TIMES ON BANKS FISHING ALL WELL

*WAITING GLOUCESTER HOME OF
DISKO TROOP WHAT SHALL DO
AND HOW IS MAMA SEND MONEY
HARVEY CHEYNE JUNIOR*

"Is it really possible?" cried Harvey Senior. "Could it really be Harvey?"

"It's the boy, sure enough," said Milsom. "I think you have found your son. Sir, we're standing by for orders."

A moment later, Harvey Cheyne was dashing up the stairs of his mansion.

"Constance! Constance! It's our son!"

* * *

"Milsom!" Mr. Cheyne commanded from the top of the stairs. "Get us to Boston as fast as you can!"

"Yes, sir!" said Mr. Milsom, rolling down the big map of American railroads that hung on the office wall. "Miss Kinzey, send these telegrams! First telegram goes to Los Angeles.

Have them send Mr. Cheyne's railroad car here to San Diego immediately!"

Soon telegrams were buzzing along the telegraph wires from coast to coast to make connections with all the different trains that would take turns pulling Mr. and Mrs. Cheyne's private railroad car. And other messages were flying around too, as Mr. Cheyne's rich enemies heard rumors that Cheyne was about to make some new move.

"What's that sly old fox up to now?" they asked each other.

Mr. Cheyne smiled grimly when he heard about the other men's panic. "Tell them all not to worry, Milsom. I'm not on the war-path now. Just tell them the truth for once. Tell them that my wife and I are on our way to see our son."

In three days and fifteen and one-half hours, the Cheynes arrived at the Boston station. Harvey was waiting for them.

* * *

Harvey feasted on food and drink as he sat with his parents in their railroad car and told of his adventures. Mr. Cheyne was used to judging men, and now he looked keenly at his son. He could see that the boy had grown. His palms were rough and hard. His arms were dotted with scars. The boy's voice was strong but respectful.

"But why didn't you tell this man, Troop, who you were?" Mrs. Cheyne asked her son.

"Disko Troop, dear," Mr. Cheyne corrected. "And he's the best man that ever walked a deck."

"But we would have paid him anything!"

"I know," said Harvey, "but he thought I was crazy, and I called him a thief because I couldn't find my money."

"A sailor found your money on the

steamer deck that night!" Mrs. Cheyne cried.

"So you see, I shouldn't have blamed Captain Troop," said Harvey. "And I don't blame him now for hitting me on the nose, either. I bled like crazy, but after that, I saw the light."

Mrs. Cheyne gasped, but Mr. Cheyne chuckled. He had never seen such a twinkle in young Harvey's eye.

"I can't do a man's work yet," said the boy, "but I can handle a dory, and I don't get scared in a fog. And I can steer, and I know my ropes. And I can pitch fish till the cows come home! I worked hard for $10.50 a month!"

"I began at $8.50 a month, my son," said Mr. Cheyne.

"Is that so, sir? You never told me."

"You never asked. I'll tell you more about it some day, if you want to know."

Harvey went on praising Disko Troop and Dan and the rest of the crew.

"I worked like a horse, and I ate like a hog, and I slept like a dead man!" he told his parents.

That was too much for Mrs. Cheyne. She remembered how she had thought of Harvey as a corpse, drowned at sea. She sobbed and went to lie down.

"I have to be getting back to Gloucester," said Harvey. "I can take a freight train. It's my job to be there tomorrow to keep count as we unload our fish."

"Well," said his father, "I think we can get this rail-car down to Gloucester as fast as your freight train. You go to bed now."

Harvey spread himself on the sofa, kicked off his boots, and was asleep before his father could turn down the lights. Mr. Cheyne sat watching the young sleeping face and began to wonder why he had ever neglected his son. "As for what I owe to Disko Troop, it's more than I could ever pay," he said.

* * *

Dan had a pretty good laugh the next day, when his father found out that Harvey really was a millionaire's son. This time, it was Disko's jaw that dropped.

"Well, then, I was mistook in my judgments," he admitted. "Don't rub it in!"

After the fish were sold and Mr. and Mrs. Cheyne got a tour of the boat, the crew was invited to see the private railroad car. They couldn't believe how fine and beautiful everything was. They were even *more* amazed when the millionaire's wife invited them to stay for dinner and then waited on them herself. That was a meal they would *never* forget.

After dinner, Mr. Cheyne and Disko sat by themselves smoking cigars.

"Tell me," said Mr. Cheyne, "what are your plans for Dan?"

"Oh, he's just a plain boy," said Disko. "He'll have the *We're Here* someday when I'm gone. But he never lets *me* do his thinkin'."

"Hmm," said Mr. Cheyne. "Ever been out West, Mr. Troop?"

"Sure, been as far west as New York City once in a boat."

"Well," said Mr. Cheyne, "I own a line of six big ships out in San Francisco, hauling tea from China. I wonder if you might lend me Dan for a year or two. I'll get my best captain to train him to a good position."

"Well, I don't know." Disko scratched his chin. "He's kind of weak on reading charts and such. It would be a risk for you to take on a boy with no experience on freighters."

Mr. Cheyne smiled. "I know a man who took a bigger risk than that."

Chapter Ten

Masters
and Men

Dan's future could not be decided
without a talk with his mother. The fathers
walked over together to the Troop's tidy
little white house. They sat down with
Mrs. Troop in the parlor and Mr. Cheyne
explained his offer.

The large, silent woman listened and said, "Tell me about these ships of yours. Do they go straight across to China and come straight back?"

"As straight as the winds will let 'em," he answered. "Mrs. Troop, my ships are strong and modern. The hulls are iron and very well built."

"Well, I can never love the sea because it took the lives of my father, my eldest brother, two nephews, and my sister's husband," she said. "But if Dan wants to go, he can," she said.

Mr. Cheyne was pleased when Dan arrived home and accepted the offer. For Dan, it was a chance that could lead to faraway ports and riches.

Mrs. Cheyne also tried to reward Manuel for fishing Harvey out of the sea, but Manuel wouldn't accept any money. Instead, he took Mrs. Cheyne to meet a priest who said she could help the church set up a fund to take care of the widows of fishermen who had been lost at sea.

As he walked around the wharf with his father, Harvey watched how well his father got along with the men they met. Mr. Cheyne had a way of speaking to someone in an honest and trusting way.

Harvey asked his father, "How do you get them to open up so and tell you what they think?"

"Well, Harve," Mr. Cheyne replied, "I've dealt with quite a few men in my time. They see that I got where I am through hard work, and they accept me as one of them."

"I'm accepted as one of them, too!" said Harvey. Then he rubbed his palms and frowned. "But, see, my hands are already getting soft again."

"That's all right," said his father. "Keep them that way for the next few years while you get your education. You can harden them up later on."

"I suppose," said Harvey with no excitement in his voice.

"Listen," said Mr. Cheyne, "you can take charge of your own life." Harvey's father held out a hand. "Play straight with me, son, and I'll play straight with you. Life's too short to waste it."

"I know I've been fooling around," said Harvey.

"Harvey," Mr. Cheyne said, "America is full of spoiled children with rich parents. Is that what you want to be? You can, you know. Or, you can work for me and earn your way."

"For how much, Dad? Ten dollars a month? I could start by sweeping the office. Isn't that how a millionaire gets started?"

"Maybe a few do," said his father. "But don't make the same mistake I made by starting too soon."

"But it made you a millionaire!"

Mr. Cheyne looked out on the water, lit a cigar, and began to tell his son the story of his life. He spoke in a low, even voice.

He told Harvey how he had begun as a boy with no family, getting in and out of trouble in mining camps all across the West. He talked about a hundred different jobs he'd had for very little pay. He talked about building and buying railroads and wrecking one, too. He talked about lumber mills and mines, and mixing with all kinds of men. He talked about men who foolishly gambled their fortunes away. He talked about times when he had hung on to his own fortune by a toenail. He talked about having the courage to beat his enemies, or to forgive them when they beat him. He told stories of other people like him who had made and lost fortunes while making the nation grow.

To Harvey, listening to his father talk this way was like watching a powerful freight train storm across the country in the dark. It stirred young Harvey's heart.

"I've never told that story to anyone before," said the father.

Harvey gasped. "It's just the greatest thing that ever was!" said he.

"I've told you what I *got* in my life, Harvey. Now I'm coming to what I *didn't* get. I didn't get an education. Harve, the future does not belong to people like me, no matter how smart we think we are. It belongs to people who are willing to learn. It belongs to those who sit down with their chins on their elbows and learn from books. Nothing pays like an education. That's why I want you to go to college."

"Four years at college?" said Harvey. "I'd rather have a ship."

"College is an investment in the future, son. Think it over, and let me know in the morning."

The following morning Harvey had a deal to offer his father. He didn't want his father's railroads or his mines.

"I'll go to college and do my best," he promised, "but I want to spend my summers on your new fleet of ships.

And when I graduate, I want you to let me run the fleet."

"It's a deal," said Mr. Cheyne at last. "When you graduate, those ships will be yours!"

"No, Dad," said Harvey. "We'll be partners. We'll run the fleet together. Disko says that families should stick together."

* * *

A few years later, a young man stood in the clammy fog outside a mansion on a street in San Francisco. As he stood by a tall iron gate, another young man rode up on a fine-looking horse.

"Hello, Dan!" said Harvey, smiling down from his saddle.

"Hello, Harve!"

"How have you been?"

"Well, they made me second mate, this trip," said Dan. "And you? Ain't you almost through with college?"

"I'm getting there. I tell you, Dan, Stanford University is nothing like the *We're Here*. I can't wait to graduate next fall!"

"Then you'll finally be master of the fleet?"

"That's right, Dan. And when I'm the boss, watch out! I'll make every man jump — including you!"

"I'll risk it," said Dan, with a brotherly grin, as Harvey got off his horse and invited Dan inside.

A man stepped out from inside the gate and took the bridle of Harvey's horse. It was MacDonald, the old cook from the *We're Here*.

"So you see, I was right," he said. "I saw it all in my dreams. Do you remember what I said, Dan Troop? Master and man. Now look who is master and who is man!"

About the Start-to-Finish Author

Alan Venable was born in Pittsburgh, Pennsylvania, in 1944 and has lived and traveled in India and other parts of Asia where Rudyard Kipling got his story ideas. Alan grew up hearing and learning Kipling's poems and stories, especially *The Jungle Book*.

Alan has written many books in the Start-to-Finish series. He has also written several books of fiction for children, textbooks for schools, and plays and novels for adults. He lives in San Francisco, a city that Kipling visited on his travels around the world.

About the Start-to-Finish Author

Jerry Stemach is a Special Educator who has worked with middle and high school students and adults learning English as a second language for more than 25 years. He has served students with language and learning disabilities as a speech and language pathologist, an assistive technology specialist, and as a special education teacher. Jerry is a member of the Start-to-Finish editing team. For the Nick Ford series, he personally visits each city, state, or country that he writes about so that he can tell the story with interesting facts.

Jerry makes his home in the Valley of the Moon in Sonoma County, California, with his wife, Beverly, and daughters, Sarah and Kristie.

About the Original Author

Rudyard Kipling (1865-1936) was born in Bombay, India, where his father was a teacher. After Kipling went to school in England, he went back to India to work. At the age of 16, he began to work for a newspaper, and soon he was writing many stories and poems about life in India. Two of his most famous books are *The Jungle Book* and *The Man Who Would Be King*. Kipling traveled to America where he met his wife. As they traveled together around the world, he began his work on this book, *Captains Courageous*. The book was published in 1897. In 1907, Rudyard Kipling got a special award for his writing. It is called the Nobel Prize for Literature.

114

About the Narrator

Todd Neumann was born and raised in Illinois. He has acted in many commercials on TV and with a comedy group in Chicago. Todd is also part of a theater group that performs murder mysteries for high school students. Todd has been acting since he was a kid. When he was in middle school he acted in two plays, and in both of them, he played a dwarf.

Todd likes to spend time with his two daughters, Lucy and Maggie. He also likes to read good books and play bad golf. He lives in Illinois with his wife, two daughters, and two basset hounds, named Jordan and Casey.